P9-AOE-092

NORTHERN LIGHTS

a Hanukkah story

by Diana Cohen Conway
illustrated by Shelly O. Haas

Kar-Ben Copies, Inc. Rockville, Maryland

PRONUNCIATION

The language spoken by Yupik Eskimos has different words and pronunciation in different villages. It's hard to know how to pronounce a language without hearing it spoken, but the guide below will give you some idea.

Yupik . . . . Yoo' pick
Assaliaq . . . . Ah·sah' lee·ack
Kuspuk . . . . Kuss' puck
Quiryak . . . . He·ur' yak

Library of Congress
Cataloging-in-Publication Data

Conway, Diana Cohen
Northern Lights: a Hanukkah story/Diana Cohen Conway: illustrated by Shelly O. Haas.
p. cm.
Summary: When a storm grounds their plane, a Jewish family celebrates Hanukkah with a Yupik Eskimo family and discovers they share many customs
ISBN 0-929371-79-8:
—ISBN 0-929371-80-1 (pbk.):
[1. Hanukkah—Fiction. 2. Eskimos—Alaska—Fiction. 3. Indians of North America—Fiction] I. Haas, Shelly O., ill. II. Title.
PZ7.C76842No 1994
[E]—dc20 94-25831
CIP
AC

Published by KAR-BEN COPIES, INC. Rockville, MD 1-800-4-KARBEN
Printed in the United States of America.

With love for my parents, Joseph and Sara
—DCC

With love to Peri
—SOH

Far north in Alaska, December is a month of darkness. The sun sleeps all day just below the horizon. Sudden winds kick snow into house-sized drifts.

One afternoon, pilot Joe Anaruk set his small plane down at the airstrip of a Yupik Eskimo village by the frozen Bering Sea.

"Blowing too hard," he told his two passengers, as he pushed open the door of the plane. "We won't fly out again until the wind lays down."

Dr. Israel pulled his hood around his face and helped his daughter down the steps. He knew storms from his many trips as a traveling doctor for the small villages.

"Then we won't get home for Hanukkah, Daddy," Sara worried aloud. It was winter vacation, and Dr. Israel had brought her with him to see new places.

"You'll stay at my mother's house while we go to the clinic," Joe reassured Sara. "She's also named Sarah. Sarah Anaruk."

A line of street lights glowed through swirling snow, reminding Sara of the silver Hanukkah menorah at home, with its curved branches.

She clung to her father's hand as they pressed against the wind, inching toward a half-buried cabin. Outside the door, a dog curled nose-to-tail raised his head and howled a warning.

Joe pushed open the door, and an elderly lady pulled them inside. She was wearing a colorful, long blouse called a *kuspuk*.

Joe introduced everyone. "My mother doesn't speak English," he explained, "but I'll send my daughter Norma over."

Dr. Israel kissed Sara goodbye. "I'll be back as soon as I've seen to the patients."

"Come back soon," she said, in her bravest-sounding voice.

Mrs. Anaruk patted the girl's red hair and then her own gray head, "Sara, Sarah," she laughed, turning to her kitchen stove.

Sara recognized the smell of oil warming in a pan. It reminded her of Hanukkah latkes frying.

"*Assaliaq*," the woman said. She pinched a ball of dough from a bowl and stretched it between her twisted fingers. The thin biscuit sizzled when she slipped it into the hot oil.

Sara thought about her family preparing for Hanukkah back home in the city. Her sister Rachel always grated the onions and potatoes for latkes. Sara's job was to beat the eggs, but her brother Mark was old enough to do that now. Her mother would mix it all together and do the frying. Sarah had never been away from home on Hanukkah before.

The cabin door burst open, and a girl in a fur parka blew in on a gust of wind. She stamped her mukluks and shook her hood, making a miniature indoor snowstorm. ''I'm Norma,'' she said, and grabbed a piece of fried bread from a plate on the stove.

''Ow, that's hot!'' she exclaimed, and broke off half for Sara. Just then the lights went out. ''Here comes the storm,'' Norma announced.

Mrs. Anaruk rattled around in the dark. A minute later a flashlight beam turned the girls into giant wall monsters.

She spoke in throaty Yupik words. Norma translated. ''Grandma says when she was little, the dark months were the time for stories.''

''I can tell you the story of Hanukkah,'' Sara offered.

''What's Hanukkah?'' Norma asked.

Sara made her shadow loom menacingly on the wall. ''This is wicked King Antiochus,'' she began. ''Long ago in a faraway land, he destroyed the Jewish Temple and made my people bow down to Greek idols.''

''Wait,'' Norma said. ''My turn.'' Norma made shadows, too, as she translated Sara's words for her grandmother.

Sara took the spatula from the stove and waved it over her head like a sword. ''The Jews fought back and drove Antiochus from the land. To give thanks that the war was over, they rebuilt the Temple and prepared to relight the menorah.''

Sara waited for Norma to repeat her words in Yupik, then lifted up the bottle of oil. "Even though they could find only a small amount of special oil for the menorah, it miraculously burned for eight nights. That's why we celebrate Hanukkah and light candles for eight nights."

With her fingers, Sara made a menorah on the wall. ''My thumb's the *shamash*, the helper candle we use to light the others. We light one candle on the first night, two the second, three the third, and so on, until we have all of them burning at once.''

When the girls finished the story, old Sarah shuffled over to the window ledge. She picked up a heavy black stone and placed it in young Sara's hands. It looked like half an avocado with the seed scooped out.

"This is an oil lamp too," Norma explained. "Long ago Yupik people burned seal oil on dark winter days."

Norma turned to her grandmother. "Do you think it still works?"

Mrs. Anaruk spooned some oil from the frying pan into the stone lamp. She tore off a narrow strip of cotton cloth from an old dish towel and twisted it into a worm-like wick.

Norma put the tail of the wick in the oil and propped its head on the edge of the stone. She handed Sara a box of wooden matches.

Sara struck one and touched it to the oil. A yellow flame darted forth, then settled to a faint blue glow. "*Baruch Atah Adonai*," she began reciting the candle-lighting prayer in Hebrew. "Blessed are You, O Lord." The light danced on the faces of the two girls.

Suddenly the door opened. ''Electricity's out all over the village,'' Joe the pilot reported as he came into the house.

''The wind blew down a pole,'' added Dr. Israel, following behind.

Sara smiled. ''Look, Daddy, we made a menorah.''

''An Eskimo menorah,'' Norma explained.

Sarah Anaruk put out plates of boiled salmon and fried bread. Norma poured hot spiced tea. The five of them ate dinner in the glow of the ancient stone lamp.

As suddenly as the wind came, it died away again. Norma and Sara looked out the window at the silent, black village, as the evening sky came alive with quivering bands of color.

"*Quiryak*," said the old woman.

"Northern lights," Joe explained.

Norma shivered. "Grandma says those are spirits that dance in the sky."

Sara hugged her new friend. "I think the heavens are lighting an enormous menorah—just for us."

ABOUT THE AUTHOR

Diana Cohen Conway came to Alaska in 1970 and taught college in Anchorage for 20 years. Now she lives on a small island in Kachemak Bay, where she grows vegetables, fishes for king salmon, and bakes sourdough bread. She has a Ph.D. in Romance Languages from New York University, and her children's fiction has appeared in several magazines. This is her first book.

ABOUT THE ILLUSTRATOR

Shelly O. Haas was raised in a home where the arts were very important. She earned a B.F.A. in Illustration from the Rhode Island School of Design. Shelly has illustrated a number of books for Kar-Ben, including *Daddy's Chair*, winner of the 1992 Sydney Taylor Award from the Association of Jewish Libraries, and *The Kingdom of Singing Birds*, which received an Honorable Mention from the Association in 1993.